The China Room

When tea first came into this country from China it was drunk from cups made in China. How did they differ from ours?

China is the popular name for PO... fine pottery which first came from...

When dinner sets wer... ordered from China, COATS OF ARMS were sent so that they could be copied onto the pieces.

This device was used to warm the glasses for red wine. It is made from a NAUTILUS shell. Who sailed in the submarine 'Nautilus'?

When Queen Elizabeth I left Berkeley Castle in a hurry she left her bedspread behind. The silver thread has now turned black. Why?

The Housekeepers' Room

The blocked up doorway was once the entrance to a passage leading to the kitchens.

Notice the unusual shape of the other doorway. This shape is only used by the Berkeley family and is called a BERKELEY ARCH.

Can you find this carving of King Neptune sitting in a shell. Why is he shown with fish and sea horses?

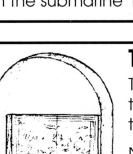

Earl Godwin is said to have owned this GODWIN CUP. How old is it?

The Beer Cellar

Beer, made in what is now the Tearoom, was piped under the courtyard to the cellar and out at this TAP.

This OSS was put under a barrel when it was in use. Why does it have steps.

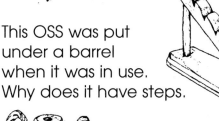

The beer was stored in these oak barrels, the large ones holding 600 gallons (2700 litres).

The barrels were made by tradesmen called COOPERS. A selection of their tools is on the wall. How do you think this one was used?

Beer in gallon jars was served to the workmen in the fields. Why do you think this beer was weaker than normal?

Notice the thickness of the CURTAIN WALLS and the narrow window slots.

The Passage

Resting in the wall, behind the door is this wooden beam. This was used to 'BAR THE DOOR'.

This PISTOL is disguised as a walking stick. Notice the small trigger. What care would the walker have to take?

The Great Hall

Enlarged in 1340, the Great Hall was the most important room in the Castle. Here people gathered to meet Lord Berkeley on business, to eat and to be entertained. The screen kept draughts out and has a gallery above from where MINSTRELS played.

The painted screen was made in the 1500s. Find the painting of the CRUCIFIXION of Jesus. The bird represents the Holy Spirit, the fish - Christianity. What does the skull represent?

A JESTER died after falling from the gallery and is buried in the churchyard. What was his name?

In the window is this shield showing the arms of a husband on the left and his wife's on the right. What were their names?

This CHANDELIER would once have held candles. What other methods of lighting would have been used?

When the Hall was built the fire would have been in the centre of the floor. A hole in the roof would have let the smoke out. Later this fireplace was put in and a raised DIAS built. The best seats would have been for Lord Berkeley and his special guests. Where would these have been?

The Grand Stairs

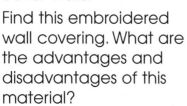

Look for this iron image of LUCIFER or the devil. For what was it used?

Many different materials have been used to cover walls.

Find this embroidered wall covering. What are the advantages and disadvantages of this material?

This is a portrait of Nell Gwynn, an actress who was a favourite of Charles II. Look for his portrait as you go round.

Berkeley Castle was built as a fortress and has had the same family living in it since Norman times. The family has gradually made it into a comfortable home over the centuries, but it is still a fortress. Situated on the banks of the River Severn it is mid-way between Gloucester and Bristol.

Look at
BERKELEY CASTLE

Earl Godwin, the father of the Saxon King Harold, had a dwelling on the site of the present castle before the Norman Conquest of 1066.

William the Conqueror gave the land to William FitzOsbern, one of his friends, who quickly built a motte and bailey wooden castle as a defence against the Welsh.

This was replaced by a stone castle in about 1088 by Roger de Berkeley and enlarged by his family over the centuries.

Edward II became King of England in 1307. He was a poor King who did not rule well and was deposed in 1327.

He was imprisoned in Berkeley Castle where he was murdered in his bed by his jailors, Sir John Maltravers and Sir Thomas Gurney.

He is buried in Gloucester Cathedral.

In 1619 a group of men from Berkeley sailed to Virginia in a small ship called "Margaret". On arrival they gave thanks to God and held the first "Thanksgiving" service in America. There is still a Berkeley village and plantation where they landed.

When the Civil War started in 1642, the family supported the King. The Castle was besieged in 1645 and after 3 days' bombardment from the church roof, surrendered. The damaged Keep wall has never been repaired.

The Baron of Berkeley was made an Earl in 1679. When the 8th Earl died in 1942 without children, the Earldom died with him but the Barony continues in the female line.

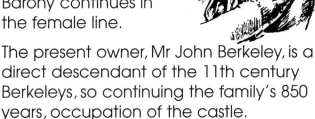

The present owner, Mr John Berkeley, is a direct descendant of the 11th century Berkeleys, so continuing the family's 850 years, occupation of the castle.

The Approach

As you climb the steps to enter the KEEP, think about the reasons for these steps. One is that the Keep was built around the mound of earth or MOTTE of the first Norman castle on this site. How would they help in its defence?

The large Norman doorway, built in the 1100s, would have allowed horsemen to ride in. As this was a weak point in the defences it was made smaller in the 1300s. Look at the Norman style of carvings.

The Kings Gallery

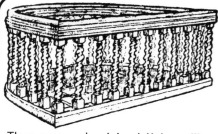

Behind these railings is the DUNGEON into which dead animals were dropped and allowed to decay. Prisoners were thrown on top and were suffocated by the gasses given off by the rotting carcases.

The room behind this grille was once larger and contained the dungeon. King Edward II was imprisoned here for many months where it was hoped that he too would die from the gasses. When he did not, he was murdered.

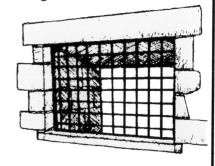

Portraits of all the Stuart Kings of England are displayed here. When did they rule?

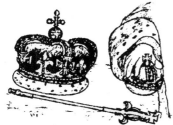

Drake's Chest is decorated with paintings of ships. This one has a BATTERING RAM fitted to its bows. Are any of the other ships fitted with this weapon?

Find the painting which shows this ROYAL REGALIA. These are the symbols of royalty. The CROWN is the symbol of authority, the SCEPTRE of power and justice and the ORB of God's domination of the world.

During the reign of Queen Elizabeth I fashionable ladies wore dresses with high collars. Would this fashion be suitable for today?

Drake's Room

TESTER BEDS were built high off the ground and often fitted with curtains to keep out draughts and for privacy. Why do you think they are no longer needed?

The TESTER above stopped 'things' falling onto the sleeper from the ceiling.

Tower Room

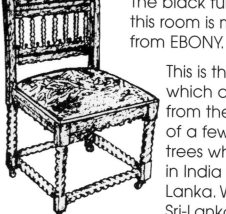

The black furniture in this room is made from EBONY.

This is the wood which comes from the centre of a few types of trees which grow in India and Sri Lanka. Where is Sri-Lanka?

Picture Gallery

Charles, Lord Berkeley was in command of this ship, the 'Tyger', in 1682 when he died. How old was he when he died?

The large red flag at the stern shows the part of the fleet or SQUADRON to which the ship belongs.

How does the ship's UNION JACK differ from today's?

Find the CAPSTAN on the model ship. This was used to lift heavy objects such as anchors. Handles were fitted into the slots and sailors pushed on these. They sang songs to help them work together. What were these called?

Look at these chairs and notice how the wooden rails have been shaped at the back to make them look very thin and delicate.

MARQUETRY is the making of patterns by inlaying pieces of one material into the surface of another.

These flowers are made from bone set into a table top. What is this bird made from and how many pieces were used?

The Dining Room

Cutlery is set on a table so that the diner uses the outside pieces first. The table is set for four courses, soup, main, dessert and cheese. Find the box in which the cutlery is stored.

Clocks had long cases to hide the weights and pendulum which made them work. The clock mechanism moved as a weight fell. This had to be wound up regularly. The length of the PENDULUM was changed to make the clock keep time.

George Berkeley, Bishop of Cloyne, left his library to the first university on the west coast of America - Berkeley University in California.

Sir William Berkeley became Governor of Virginia in 1641. What is a GOVERNOR?

The Game Larder

Most farm animals had to be killed in the autumn as they could not be fed over the winter. GAME was an important fresh meat in winter and it was illegal for ordinary people to catch it. What is poaching?

If FOXHOUNDS hunted foxes and DEERHOUNDS hunted deer, what did GREYHOUNDS hunt?

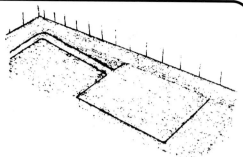

Notice the grooves on the floor. Why do you think they were needed?

The Buttery

A fire was lit in this now blocked up BREAD OVEN and removed when the oven was hot enough to bake bread. How did they put the bread into the oven without getting burnt?

A MORTAR and PESTLE were used to crush food into small   pieces

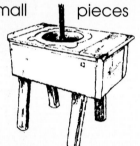

The frame was used to hang LAMPREY from when they were being smoked. What other ways were used to preserve food before the refrigerator was invented?

How is this done today?

Water used in these lead lined sinks came from a well under the courtyard. Can you think how?

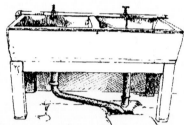

These bells were fitted to waggons, each set making a different sound.

Why did each waggon need to have a different set?

The Kitchen

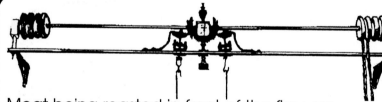

Meat being roasted in front of the fire was turned on the SPIT. The spit was rotated by a fan in the chimney which was turned by the rising hot air from the fire. Look for the bar coming from the chimney and work out how this works.

This plate is made from a mixture of lead and tin called PEWTER. Why are plates not made of pewter today?

Pans were made of COPPER because heat passes through this metal easily. From what material would you make the handle?

Meat pies were made in this BRASS mould. How were they removed without breaking?

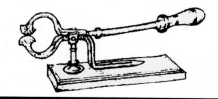

Sugar was bought in solid cones called SUGAR LOAVES. This cutter was used to cut pieces off. How would these pieces be crushed for use?

Morning Room

How do you think looking at this carving would help you to decide when the room was built?

The SUN DIAL set into the window could only have been used when the sun shone. What other reason can you think of which would prevent its use for part of the year?

The lines on which music is written are called the STAFF. How does the music in the glass case differ from today's?

Carvings of animals, or parts of animals, were often used to decorate the legs of furniture. On which piece is this lion?

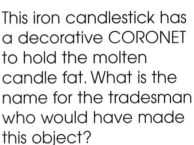

This iron candlestick has a decorative CORONET to hold the molten candle fat. What is the name for the tradesman who would have made this object?

The Long Drawing Room

Mary Cole, a local butcher's daughter, is said to have secretly married the 5th Earl of Berkeley twelve years before the official wedding.

Because this was not believed, their eldest son was not allowed to inherit the title.

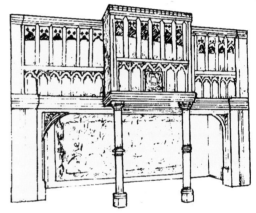

This adjustable POLE SCREEN kept the heat of the fire from ladies' faces. Their make-up was made of wax. What happened if it got warm?

This gallery, or KING'S PEW, was made to fit into the Morning Room when that room was the castle's chapel. Mass could last many hours and here in the privacy of the gallery the occupants might doze off.

The Small Drawing Room

Through the large window look across the meadows to the New Kennels built in 1730, and beyond to the Deer Park. There have been hounds here since Norman times, and Queen Elizabeth I came here to hunt.

The Berkeley Hunt wears yellow livery. What colour do other hunts wear?

The wall TAPESTRIES show scenes from the stories by Ovid, the Roman poet, about Greek and Roman heroes. Look to see how a tapestry is made.

Personal SEALS were used instead of signatures when most people could not write. This one was used by Edward II on State documents. Why was wax a suitable material for seals?

Can you find the maker's name woven into the carpet?

Inner Courtyard

The KEEP is the oldest part of the Castle. The courtyard or BAILEY was later surrounded by a CURTAIN WALL with a walkway at the top. When more comfort was wanted, rooms were built against this wall. Why would the walkway be needed?

Archers used these slots to fire through.

How were they shaped to allow arrows to be fired downwards?

The room over the steps to the Keep was that in which Edward II was murdered. Can you identify the other rooms through which you have passed from the courtyard?

This MOUNTING BLOCK was used to help riders mount their horses. Which way did the horse face?

Look at the door of this tower, with its carvings of saints. Can you see that of the patron saint of Scotland, St Andrew?

Outer Courtyard

The family has a tradition that a seed or cutting from a tree is brought back from any battlefield on which they have fought. This SCOTS PINE came from the Field of Flodden. Where and when was this battle?

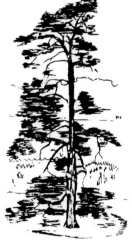

Try to imagine yourself attacking this castle. No doubt a rider would have been sent to open the dykes to flood the land on which this view of the castle is seen. How would you, with the medieval weapons, set about its capture?

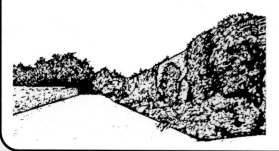

This BOWLING GREEN dates from the 1500s. Who was playing bowls when the Armada was sighted?

Game caught on the estate was hung in this house before being taken into the Castle. What were its windows made from?

Published and copyright © 1992, this revision 2005 by Bessacarr Publications Ltd.
No. 4925067 Reg. Off. 3 Highfield, Hatton Park, Warwick CV35 7TQ. +44 (0)1926 402055
www.bessacarr.com   Send SAE for our publications list

ISBN 086384261-5